This

Ladybird first favourite tale

belongs to

...

Published by Ladybird Books Ltd
A Penguin Company
Penguin Books Ltd, 80 Strand, London WC2R 0RL, UK
Penguin Books Australia Ltd, Camberwell, Victoria, Australia
Penguin Group (NZ) 67 Apollo Drive, Rosedale, North Shore 0632, New Zealand

001 – 10 9 8 7 6 5 4 3 2 1

© Ladybird Books Ltd MCMXCIX
This edition MMXII

ISBN: 978-1-40930-957-4

Printed in China

Ladybird First Favourite Tales

The Enormous Turnip

BASED ON A TRADITIONAL FOLK TALE

retold by Irene Yates ★ illustrated by Jan Lewis

Once, a man came out to his garden with his turnip seeds and his hoe. He dug and he delved and he set his seeds in a row.

He cared for his seeds and watered them well, and the turnip seeds began to ...

swell...

In a very few days came little green leaves.
They poked and they pushed and they
pointed. The man with the hoe rolled up
his sleeves...

That's a weed!

He plucked out the weeds and raked off the rubble.
He didn't know there was going to be trouble.

At last the turnips began to grow. They got bigger and bigger and bigger.

And the man with the hoe said, "So ... we'll have turnips for breakfast and lunch and for tea. And it's turnips for supper, too, thanks to me."

One of the turnips — the best of the lot — began to take over the whole of his plot.

Look at that one!

It grew bigger and bigger every day.
It was huge. It was vast. It was . . .

ENORMOUS!

The other poor turnips got out of its way.

The man was baffled but he kept on hoeing.
And the ENORMOUS turnip kept on growing.

The man thought it must be time at last to pull the turnip, but it just stuck fast.

"Come and help heave!" called the man to his wife.

The man pulled the turnip and the wife pulled the man. But the ENORMOUS turnip just wouldn't budge!

Heave!

"Come and help heave!" called the wife to a boy.

The man pulled the turnip, the wife pulled the man, the boy pulled the wife.

All together!

But the ENORMOUS turnip just wouldn't budge!

"Come and help heave!" called the boy to a girl.

The man pulled the turnip, the wife pulled the man, the boy pulled the wife, the girl pulled the boy.

But the ENORMOUS turnip just wouldn't budge!

One, two, three . . . !

"Come and help heave!" called the girl to
a dog.

The man pulled the turnip, the wife pulled
the man, the boy pulled the wife, the girl
pulled the boy, the dog pulled the girl.

But the ENORMOUS turnip just wouldn't budge!

Woof!

"Come and help heave!" called the dog to a cat.

The man pulled the turnip, the wife pulled the man, the boy pulled the wife, the girl pulled the boy, the dog pulled the girl, the cat pulled the dog.

Miaow!

But the ENORMOUS turnip just wouldn't budge!

"Come and help heave!" called the cat to a mouse.

The man pulled the turnip, the wife pulled the man, the boy pulled the wife, the girl pulled the boy, the dog pulled the girl, the cat pulled the dog, the mouse pulled the cat and . . .

...the ENORMOUS turnip shot right out with a *THUD!* and a *THWACK!* and a *THUMP!* And they all fell back, with a ...

Bump...

Whoops!

Ouch!

Then it was turnip for breakfast and lunch and for tea, and turnip for supper and ... oh, deary me!

Anyone for seconds?

The turnip's so good that they can't get their fill
and it's just so ENORMOUS they're eating it still!